Cinnamon Goes Over the Edge

Written by
Susan Paroff and Alli Caudle

Illustrated by
Erin Nielson

Once upon a time, there was a hedge on the edge of a yard.
There were strict rules and laws enforced by the guards.

"Set your alarms. Go to bed at sunrise!
Keep to yourselves, we're watching you guys."

And then, there was Cinnamon.
She was different, spunky and spicy.
She was fired up to dance,
and asked everyone nicely.

"Will you dance with me?"
"No thanks," said Coco.

Champagne said, *"Scram."*

She even asked the Mayor
and he said,

"No ma'am!"

"But I feel something's missing.
There's a hole in my heart,
and only a friend could fill up this part."

So, she sang, and she tapped, and she clapped very loud,
hoping that someone would step out of the crowd.
But the guards approached her, pointing to the sign:

"No parties, no dancing, and stay in line!"

She cried and she cried, while pointing her toes,
as she spun through her thoughts, thinking nobody knows…

"There's a world over there, not so far away.
These rules are wrong. I'll prove it today!"

She picked up her acorn, and waited til' dawn.
She could no longer abide by rules that felt wrong.
She said to her acorn, *"We're just a couple of nuts."*
She knew it was time to go with her guts.

So, she climbed to the tippy top of the hedge.
How scary it was to be out on the edge.
With her nut in her pack, there was no turning back.
She hung on a branch that blew in the wind,
"I'm going out there to find a true friend!"

And with one big leap, she flew through the air,
happy and free, without a care.

She envisioned she was
a superhero with a golden cape.

Little did she know
that she'd land near a snake!

She slid on her belly and they met face-to-face.

"Please don't eat me," he begged her, *"I'm not good to taste!"*

"Surely I won't eat you! I'm just looking to dance."

"How 'bout a tomato?" as he put her in a trance …

Entranced, she fell into a fog, and dreamt that
Champagne and Coco were her bestie hedgehogs.
Their friendship had power from the moon to the stars.
They were unstoppable; they were superstars!

While Cinnamon snored, her mouth made a bubble,
that popped as she was scooped up by a shovel.

She woke up in the dirt as a wheelbarrow rolled.
An earth worm inched towards her with a smile so bold.

*"Funny meeting you here.
What is the chance?"*

*"Good morning, cute earth worm.
Would you like to dance?"*

The earth worm nodded his head saying *yes*,
as a bird snatched him up and took him to its nest.

Cinnamon started to panic with her spikes in a bunch.
"I hope that bird doesn't eat him for lunch!"

Her eyes swelled up like red jelly beans.
She started to feel angry because life was so mean.
She questioned why she wasn't like all the rest,
but she said to herself, *"Be strong, this is just a test."*

She swayed and she shook from the right to the left,
and when the wheelbarrow stopped, she no longer wept.
She stood up to dust the dirt off her shoulders,
as Franny the fox jumped down from a boulder.

"Well hello, little delicious one.
I'm going to eat you. Yum, yum, yum!
I'll pick off every single spike,
so I can savor every bite."

Her heart started racing. Her mind did a twirl.
"How could I have been such a foolish girl?"
She wished she had listened to the guards and their laws,
'cause now she was a ball inside Franny's sharp claws!

"OUUUUCHHHH!!!!"

Franny screamed as she howled to the sky.

"That big queen bee stung me right in the eye!"

Cinnamon fell from her grip to the ground,
rolling and rolling, not making a sound.

She felt so homesick, she reached for her nut.
She held it tight and said, *"I'll get us out of this rut."*
She missed the hedge and wondered what life was like.
"Does anyone miss me? Are they glad I took a hike?"

"Have you seen Cinnamon?" Champagne asked Coco.

"No, I haven't seen her. Why, where did she go?"

"She's not sleeping, not dancing, I've even asked
Dr. Brown. He said he hadn't seen her around."

"Oh, that's strange! She's always bugging everyone,
wanting to dance, and having so much fun."

"But is it such a bad thing to be silly and play?"

"Yes, I think so. At least that's what they say!"

SPLASH!

WOOSH!

Cinnamon landed in the sea of a giant puddle owned by Mr. McGee.

SLOP!

LICK!

"Stop! I'm not a stick! Put me down, silly dog! Can't you see I'm a hedgehog?"

"I know," said the dog, "I have a friend upstairs. You'll meet her right now. She's combing her hairs."

Plop! She dropped to the bottom of a cage …

"Doesn't she look awesome? Everybody clap!
Here you go, look at your reflection.
Don't you love all that perfection?"

"I don't recognize myself. I think I look funny.
I look like a fish, or maybe a bunny!"

Cinnamon started crying, her tears fell to the floor.

"I want to go home. Where is the door?"

"Sorry you feel that way. It's just so tragic.
I wanted to help you, and give you my magic."

"I don't need your magic, I just want a pal.
Everyone needs one, all guys and all gals.
Will I ever have one? Are they so hard to find?
Someone who's friendly, someone who's kind.
Someone to laugh with, and dance with all night long,
to share funny stories, and sing silly songs.
A true friend to share secrets and never feel alone,
to help us face our fears and be brave on our own."

"Wow! My likes just went to two million and two!
I think I should post a lot more of you.
Oh, look, there's Mr. McGee!
He'll make you a star, just like me."

Cinnamon rolled up in a ball, oh so tight,

while Champagne and Coco stirred up a fight.

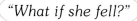

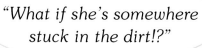

As Mr. McGee brought Cinnamon to his truck,
he said, *"Two hedgehogs, oh, what luck!"*
He couldn't wait to show his wife,
but Cinnamon jumped with all her might!
She rolled and she rolled faster than a train,
and landed in a stinky, muddy terrain.

*"Just when I thought things couldn't get worse.
I can't take any more. My heart's gonna burst!"*

She shook, and she cried, and she started to panic.
She felt out of sorts, and all kinds of manic.

*"I'll never get home. I'll never find a friend!
Will my loneliness stop? Will my pain ever end?"*

Defeated, she slumped towards the huge forest trees.
She looked up so lost, *"They'll never find me."*

"What do you mean? You're not so hard to find.
In fact, you were just on my mind.
I was hoping for a tasty dish.
Why, little hedgehog, do you look like a fish?
Your lips are so big.
Are you wearing a wig?"

"It's a long story, too long to tell.
Things really haven't been going so well.
If you want to eat me, just go ahead, chew.
'Cause right at this moment,
I don't know what to do."

Champagne and Coco gathered the troops,
and built a giant rope with 100 loops.
They looped a loop around each of their bellies,
and held on real tight, and held on real steady.
They lowered down the hedge one by one,
marching together, into the sun.

"Even though we may be breaking a rule,
it's to save our friend, so we think it's cool!"

Oh, they were scared, chanting with fear.

"I hope that she's close, I hope that she's near!"

And near Cinnamon was to Franny's sharp fangs.

"You look delicious, did you always have bangs?"

"You know what, Franny, I've learned a lot on this ride.
I've learned to be myself. I have nothing to hide.
I just wanted a friend to dance with and play,
but I'm all I've got at the end of the day."

"Sway to the left, sway to the right, boogy on down and hold on tight!
Sway to the left, sway to the right, boogy on down and hold on tight!"

"Wait, did I just hear Champagne and Coco?"

"Sounds to me like a bunch of rodents going loco."

"Put down our friend!" the hogs all shouted.

"Me?"

"Yeah, you! Friendship should never be doubted."

"You mean we're friends?
Is this really true?"

"Yes, Cinnamon! We've come to save you!
It's time to go home now. Here take a knot!
We've really missed you a whole, whole lot."

"But I broke the rules, and put you at risk."
"Hahaha! Tisk, tisk,tisk."
"Who says a rule can't be changed? If its purpose is good, it can be rearranged."

"Hoo-Hoo! Did someone call my name?"
asked the majestic white owl.
"They call me the Great Dame.
Mrs. Fox, we meet again."

"We sure do, my fine-feathered friend."

"Put down that hedgehog, you must let her go!
This forest needs peace, don't you know?
We're here to protect all that is good.
Remember, Mrs. Fox, it's everyone's neighborhood."

The owls spread their wings, as Cinnamon started to sing …

"Hummmm we ain't gonna run,
so we're gonna back this up."

And everybody said, "YUPPP!"

The hogs started to dance real, real slow,
hoping that Franny would just let her go.
The owls joined in tune,
it was a cascade of croons.
They circled and swirled around Franny the fox,
as Cinnamon escaped Franny shouted, "Stop!"

She bounced into the hogs' warm embrace.

"I've missed you so much. Let's get out of this place!"

"Not so fast," said a papa bear and his baby bear cub.
"Got a sandwich to share? Or maybe a hug?"

"That's sweet, Mr. Bear, but we've gotta run."

"Cinnamon, your acorn. Turn around, hun!"

"I don't need it anymore. I'm safe on my own."

"Hurry up guys, we've gotta get home!"

They climbed up the fence and over the hedge,
happy and safe, back from the edge.
The sun started rising. It was almost time for bed.

"We're not that tired. Let's dance instead!"

Cinnamon, Champagne and Coco
hugged really hard,
while everyone danced, including the guards.

"Some rules are clear, and some rules are cloudy.

Some keep you safe, and some make you pouty.

Some rules teach you how to be a good friend.

Some rules are silly, and some rules we bend."

The mayor listened and nodded his head. He thought for a moment, smiled and said …

"All rules are up for interpretation, and seeing your passion gives me much inspiration! We must be careful and thoughtful in our space, but maybe sometimes we can dance in place!"

The hedgehogs all smiled, they hugged, and they cheered!
"Thank you, Cinnamon! You've made it better here!"
They put their paws in the air, and shimmied their bums.
The music started playing … humm, humm humm!

THE END!

About the Authors

Susan Paroff is a music composer and writer who values learning through experiences. As a mother of two, she knows the importance of sharing our unique stories and learning from each other. She believes art is not only the path to healing ourselves, but our greater community. Her works can be heard on: Disney, Nickelodeon, Netflix, as well as off-Broadway and feature films. Susan resides in New York City with her husband, two children, and dogs in a busy, fun-filled home; where she takes time to sing and dance everyday.

Alli Caudle, a life coach, writer and producer, has taken her creativity to a new level with *Cinnamon Goes Over the Edge*. Combining her love for children and her passion for mental health, Alli tackles some of the biggest issues children face today. She reminds her readers that within our community, the greatest healing can transpire when we open our hearts and minds with a little fun! Alli works alongside her mother at Sotheby's International Realty in Dallas, TX; where she lives with her dog, Buddy, who teaches her something new about love every day.

Archway Publishing books may be ordered through booksellers or by contacting:

Archway Publishing
1663 Liberty Drive
Bloomington, IN 47403
www.archwaypublishing.com
844-669-3957

ISBN: 978-1-6657-2024-3 (sc)
978-1-6657-2025-0 (hc)
978-1-6657-2092-2 (e)

Print information available on the last page.

Archway Publishing rev. date: 06/28/2022